Tu Meke Tūi!

**For Jasper and anyone
who ever wanted to fly**

Tumeke is a New Zealand Māori word which
means to startle or take fright.

In recent years, *tu meke* (as two words) has
developed as a colloquial phrase meaning
'too much' and is used to express excitement
or being shaken up.

Malcolm Clarke

Tu Meke Tūi!

There's more to being a bird than flying

Illustrated by

FLOX

Deep in the forest at the
first sign of light,
Tere the Tūī set off on
her flight.

But as she was tumbling
around in the sun,
she couldn't help feeling a
little ho-hum.

For as much as she loved to
soar and to sing,
she desperately wanted a
friend to join in.

It was then that she noticed
way down, far below,
a stocky blue bird eating
grass with his toes.

With a flounce and a flutter, Tere tooted, "Oh, hey!"
Then she swooped down beside him, fluting, "How is your day?"

"It's good," said the bird, "and I'm pleased to meet you. I'm Taitū the Takahē. How do you do?"

Taitū shook his head as he
lowered his beak
and explained to Tere that
his wings were too weak.

"You needn't be scared,
my new friend, Taitū,
I'll teach you to fly, high
up in the blue."

"Stand on that rock and flap
your wings fast.
Take a big jump and you'll
be flying at last."

Taitū's knees knocked and he
was trembling badly
as he jumped off the rock and
flapped his wings madly.

But while little Tere was focused on coaching, Stan the sly Stoat was quickly approaching.

As Taitū fell down with a
thundering crash,
Stan careened forward, hissing,
"REOWCATTASHHH!"

Stan was too quick and poor
Tere was stuck.
She screeched and she flapped
her wings with no luck.

Then Taitū stood up and
with all of his might,
raised a leg in the air and
kicked Stan far from sight.

With a sigh of relief Tere brushed herself clean. "Taitū, you're the bravest bird I've ever seen."

"Oh, tu meke, Tere! There's
just one thing,
I know I can't fly, but
instead could we sing?"

"Oh, yes," answered Tere, "that
would be fun!"
And they burst into song beneath
the warm morning sun.

Tere the Tūī

Taitū the Takahē

Monique the Monarch Butterfly

Tahi the Tuatara

Did you spot…?

There are more forest friends hiding in the pages, take a look back through the book and see if you can find them.

Keri the Kōtare

Katie the Kahukura Butterfly

Kelly the Kererū

Pania the Pīwakawaka

ABOUT THE AUTHOR

Creativity is only limited by the power of imagination and since he was young Malcolm Clarke has worked to push his imagination to its full potential. As an editor for television Malcolm has worked internationally with some of the best in the business while maintaining a steady passion for a wide variety of creative pursuits such as writing, acting, theatre and film projects.

The idea for *Tu Meke Tūī!* was born out of Malcolm's appreciation for New Zealand's native wildlife and his desire to expose young readers to the wonders of the natural world.

ABOUT THE ILLUSTRATOR

A graffiti artist with a fine arts degree, Flox first made her mark in inner-city Auckland, New Zealand, her trademark native birds, ferns and flowers magically transforming grey walls into vibrant depictions of nature.

Now seen everywhere from Berlin, Hong Kong and New York to Taiwan, the artist is certainly spreading her wings.

www.flox.co.nz

ACKNOWLEDGEMENTS

This project would never have taken flight had it not been for the dedication and support of Sophia Egan-Reid and Anna Egan-Reid from Mary Egan Publishing.

Gratitude and love also to Willow Sherwood, Kyle Mewburn, Sara-May Buchanan, Janelle Bish, Rita Attwood, Evelyn Tobin and Louise Russell.

For information on how to help protect New Zealand's native forest and birds please visit: **www.forestandbird.org.nz**

little
love

Published by Little Love, an imprint of Mary Egan Publishing
www.maryegan.co.nz
www.facebook.com/maryeganpublishing
www.facebook.com/tumeketui

This edition published 2017

Designer: Anna Egan-Reid
Project Manager: Sophia Egan-Reid
Kaiwhakamāori: E M Winiana.o Ngāti Manu, Ngāpuhi

Printed in China

ISBN 978-0-473-40289-1